MIDNIGHT
IN
MEMPHIS

First published in Great Britain 1998
This edition published 2002
by Egmont Books Limited
239 Kensington High Street, London W8 6SA
Published in hardback by Heinemann Library,
a division of Reed Educational and Professional Printing Ltd
by arrangement with Egmont Books Limited
Text copyright © Tony Bradman 1998
Illustrations copyright © Martin Chatterton 1998
The author and the illustrator have asserted their moral rights
Paperback ISBN 1 4052 0254 8
Hardback ISBN 0 434 80208 5
10 9 8 7 6 5 4 3 2 1
A CIP catalogue record for this title
is available from the British Library
Printed and bound in the U.A.E

MIDNIGHT
IN
MEMPHIS

WRITTEN BY TONY BRADMAN
ILLUSTRATED BY MARTIN CHATTERTON
COLOURED BY ANN CHATTERTON

BLue Bananas

To our Mummies
(and our Daddies)
M.C.

For
Ramona
T.B.

It was night time in The Land of Sand, and all the stars were twinkling. (Isn't that one twinkling a bit too brightly? Maybe not!)

It was quiet by the palm trees . . .

quiet at the

mummy police

station . . .

quiet in Memphis . . .

and quiet by

the pyramid.

(Isn't that star getting bigger and bigger?

Maybe not!)

And deep inside the pyramid it was very quiet indeed. For that's where a family of mummies was fast asleep!

But not for long . . .

In the morning the Mummies were going

on holiday. But now they were dreaming.

Then Daddy Mummy started to snore.

Soon there was another noise, too.

And suddenly there was a very loud . . .

The pyramid rocked, and everybody woke up. The Mummies hugged each other in fright.

The Mummies went to the front door,
and stepped into the night.
A strange light shone down.

They looked up and saw . . .

a flying saucer! And it was sitting

on the top of the pyramid!

Lots of little green people came out of the flying saucer. The Mummies couldn't understand them. But they seemed very nice. There was a man with them too, and he was pretty confused.

Er...like have we landed yet?

Bibble!

Shmibble!

Bobble!

Dobble!

Guff!

Spooch!

The Mummies introduced themselves.

Then the Mummies discovered something

very odd. The man couldn't remember

his name, or where he lived.

Mummy Mummy and Daddy Mummy

felt sorry for him . . .

. . . and said he could stay until his

memory returned. That pleased

the little green people.

They climbed into their flying saucer and left with a great big . . .

WHOOSH!

But when the sand settled . . .

. . . the Mummies were rather taken

aback. The pyramid looked different.

In fact it had a GIGANTIC crack!

In the morning, the Mummies got up and . . . didn't go on holiday. Mummy Mummy and Daddy Mummy tried to tidy up. Their guest just sat there whistling.

Mummy Mummy and Daddy Mummy

tried to fix the crack.

But it was just too difficult. So they

decided to call . . .

The Concrete Sisters. Their names were Cleo, Pat and Nefertiti . . . and they were the best builders in The Land of Sand.

They came . . .

they tutted . . .

they measured . . .

they muttered . . .

and they shook their heads.

Then they wrote out an estimate.

The Concrete Sisters got
started straight away.

DRRR! DRRR! DRRR!

they went

with their big drills.

BANG! BANG! BANG!

they went

with their

big

hammers.

DRRR! DRRR! DRRR!

they went with their big drills

again. But somebody

seemed to enjoy the

noise.

Mummy Mummy and Daddy Mummy
felt very fed up.

They wished they were on holiday.

Their guest still couldn't remember

anything.

And The Concrete Sisters were making a terrible mess.

The Mummy kids were having fun,
though. They did lots of helping . . .
and lots of getting in the way.

Then Tut and Sis found some old bandages, and soon The Concrete Sisters were very wrapped up in their work!

That was enough for the Mummies. They
decided it was time to take their guest out.
So they all jumped in the mummy car.

Their guest hummed along to the

mummy radio . . .

. . . and they drove to the mummy police station.

Mummy Mummy asked if anyone had reported a missing man. But the mummy cops couldn't help. They only dealt with missing mummies, not musical men with missing memories.

It was true, their guest was very musical . . .

The Mummies looked at each other.

They were in complete harmony.

And now they knew where to go. They got everybody back into the mummy car and headed for . . . Memphis.

They went straight to the mummy music

store. Tut and Sis ran in . . .

. . . and soon saw who their guest was!

The picture on the record cover struck a

chord with him, too.

His name was Axle Grease, and he was a

star - a rock and roll one.

Axle remembered that he

had fallen over and bumped his head.

And that had made him

lose his memory.

The little green people had found him

 wandering around, and taken

him for a ride.

He'd had a great time

with them. But he was glad to have his

memory back.

Axle was grateful to the Mummies for helping him. So later that evening, he gave a concert at the mummy music store.

It was midnight at Memphis, and everybody was there. Axle had a backing band that was way beyond compare.

The Concrete Sisters playing, the Mummies singing too, rocking and a-rolling with a mummy shoo-be-doo.

The concert was a great success. In fact, they made enough money to re-build the pyramid . . .

That wasn't all, though. Axle said the Mummies deserved a holiday . . . and he arranged one for them. He took them to the mummy airport himself.

He seemed very happy indeed . . .

And suddenly Mummy

Mummy and Daddy

Mummy realised . . .

43

. . . they were on board the flying saucer with the little green people! The door started closing before they could get off.

45

And that's the end of the story.

HEAVERS FARM PRIMARY SCHOOL
58 Dinsdale Gardens
South Norwood
SE25 6LT
Tel: 020 8653 5434 Fax: 020 8653 8055
Email: chris.heaversfarm@rmplc.co.uk